Lan~~guage~~

Story Keeper Series
Book 11

Dave and Pat Sargent (*left*) are longtime residents of Prairie Grove, Arkansas. Dave, a fourth-generation dairy farmer, began writing in early December of 1990. Pat, a former teacher, began writing in the fourth grade. They enjoy the outdoors and have a real love for animals.

Sue Rogers (*right*) returned to her beloved Mississippi after retirement. She shared books with children for more than thirty years. These stories fulfill a dream of writing books—to continue the sharing.

Land of the Sun

Story Keeper Series
Book 11

Dave and Pat Sargent
and Sue Rogers

Beyond "The End"
By Sue Rogers

Illustrated by Jane Lenoir

Ozark Publishing, Inc.
P.O. Box 228
Prairie Grove, AR 72753

Cataloging-in-Publication Data

Sargent, Dave, 1941–
    Land of the sun / by Dave and
Pat Sargent and Sue Rogers ; illustrated by
Jane Lenoir. —Prairie Grove, AR : Ozark
Publishing, c2005.
        p. cm. (Story keeper series ; 11)

    "Respect elders"—Cover.
    SUMMARY: A little Ute girl and her
grandfather stand together on the soft earth
and watch the morning sun dance in the
dewdrops. In an unselfish act she gives up
her chance to have a white rabbit fur robe.
    ISBN 1-56763-923-2 (hc)
            1-56763-924-0 (pbk)

1. Indians of North America—Juvenile
fiction. 2. Ute Indians—Juvenile fiction.
[1. Native Americans—United States—Fiction.
2. Ute Indians—Fiction.] 1. Sargent, Pat, 1936–
II. Rogers, Sue, 1933– III. Lenoir,
Jane, 1950– ill. IV. Title. V. Series.
    PZ7.S243La 2005
    [Fic]—dc21   2003090098

Printed in the United States of America

iv

Inspired by

a creation legend of the Ute people.

Dedicated to

children who are eager to learn more about the cultures of the first people who lived in this land.

Foreword

Chumani is a Ute girl who wants a new white rabbit fur robe. To make her dancing eyes happy again, GrandGrand takes up his old trade of trapping. Chumani and GrandGrand both work hard, but before the robe is finished, GrandGrand is possessed by an evil spirit and cannot get well. What can Chumani do to help her grandfather?

Contents

If you would like to have the authors of the Story Keeper Series visit your school, free of charge, just call us at 1-800-321-5671 or 1-800-960-3876.

One

Dewdrops

In the long ago, Manitou, the Great Spirit, made a hole in the sky. He swept the dirt and stones from his floor through the hole. The rocks made great mountains on the earth below. The dirt made rolling plains. It was a beautiful place. He made trees, flowers, animals, birds, and the Ute people to live there. Ute means "land of the sun".

GrandGrand told us the story of our people when we were first tucked in our cradleboards. He told it again when the sleeping Ute Mountain was wearing his big green spring blanket.

And again when the summer blanket changed to a dark green. He repeated it when we saw the red and yellow fall blanket and when the white winter blanket wrapped the mountain.

Our tipi was filled with stories during the cold winter. GrandGrand sat by the fire. We gathered around him, bundled in rabbit robes.

Snow drifted in under the tipi through little gaps. We rushed to cover the drafts. Then we waited eagerly for him to begin.

There were tales of courage about our fathers protecting us from our enemies. We heard of their bravery during the fall hunts. He told about the gathering of the clans for the Bear Dance and how my mother chose a tall handsome man from a southern clan to dance with one spring. He lived in a brush wickiup.

The man's family soon moved away and left the house! We had so many questions. But we did not talk. We were rewarded with a story of Mother and Father's wedding later that summer. Story after story—but always there was the story of how the Utes first came to be.

Then GrandGrand looked up and said, "The Jack Rabbit (big dipper) points to bedtime for boys and girls." Soon the tipi was quiet.

We never tired of hearing these stories of our people. We watched for clouds to gather on top of the highest mountain peak. It meant our ways were pleasing. Rain would slip from Manitou's pockets to make the earth more beautiful.

Early morning was my favorite time in summer. GrandGrand and I slipped out each morning to see the shiny dewdrops.

"The morning sun dances in the dewdrops. See them sparkle," said GrandGrand. "Your eyes dance too, my happy child."

My heart was warmed. We stood together on the soft earth.

My name is Chumani, which means dewdrops. I have traveled with my family seven seasons. Our tipi lay under elk robes my father had hunted.

GrandMama and GrandGrand watched us play while both Mother and Father gathered and hunted food.

GrandMama taught the girls to do chores to help our mother. We learned to dig roots, find berries, carry water, and gather wood.

The boys learned to hunt deer and antelope. They learned to clear a new campground for our tipis.

GrandMama taught us that the oldest person of the family was served first. We must never take a drink before an older person. It was bad manners to speak before the oldest person.

We were never spanked. We had been warned that an evil spirit would come and get us if we misbehaved.

We moved to a new place when GrandGrand announced, "There is no more food here. We must go to the next place."

We had our own favorite trails through the tall mountains. We had hidden berry patches and hunting grounds. While the women looked for berries, onions, and other types of food, the men hunted and fished.

Two

White-tailed Jacks

"Father," I asked, "How many rabbit pelts will it take to make a robe for me?"

"You have a warm robe now, my little dewdrop," said Father.

"Yes, Father. I have thanked the spirits many times for it," I said. "My older brothers and sisters have all used my robe. Macawi left berry stains on the front of the robe. And do you remember when Ohitekah sat on the hot coal and burned his leg? The hot coal burned the robe first. Oh Father, I would so like a white rabbit fur robe!"

"There will be no white rabbits until the snows come," said Father.

"I will wait, Father. Then I will have learned to do almost everything Mother does. I will cook rabbit stew with wild onions, Father!" I said.

"Hmm," said Father. No more was said. My heart was sad.

We moved to the piñon forests in the fall and gathered nuts that came from the pine cones of this tree. Camp was set up in the pines.

"Come, Chumani, you are old enough to help gather piñon nuts," said my mother. "GrandMama has made a basket for you."

The nuts fell out of the pine cones when they were ripe. We hurried to gather them before the squirrels got them. Father and other tall men sometimes had to knock the nuts

down from the trees with sticks. Our
baskets filled quickly at first.

We gathered piñon nuts until it turned very cold. Snow would soon come to the high country where the piñon trees grew. We moved to our winter camp in the warmer flatlands.

Mother put our winter supply of seeds, roots, pine nuts, and dried berries in storage pits that my older sisters dug. They hung jerky from poles. They piled meat on willow racks at the top of our tipi. They stored willows for making baskets. They also stored large bundles of rabbit pelts for making robes and blankets. There were no white pelts.

"What are those dancing eyes of your searching for, Chumani?" asked GrandGrand. "Your eyes do not look happy today."

"Oh, GrandGrand," I said in a worried voice, "With all my heart I

want a white rabbit fur robe. I asked
Father, but he said I already had a
warm robe."

"Hmm," said GrandGrand.

Preparing for winter was a very busy time. I was now old enough to have extra duties. There was little time for me to think of a new robe. But always, in my dreams, I wore a beautiful white rabbit fur robe!

One day GrandGrand and I were in the forest. We heard a soft thump, thump, thump.

"Listen Chumani," whispered GrandGrand. "It sounds like a rabbit thumping its hind feet on the ground. It senses our presence. It must be telling the others of danger."

Then, suddenly, out of a clump of weeds, ran four white bunnies and a white-tailed jack. Their speed was broken by long leaps.

"Look, GrandGrand! Do you see? The bunnies are wearing their winter white fur!" I said.

"Those bunnies put the dancing back in your eyes, my happy child," said GrandGrand. "You will have your new white robe."

The Poowagudt told my uncles that they must take GrandGrand to Yampa. "Only there in the waters of the hot springs flowing through the sacred caves can the evil spirit be driven out," they said.

It was easy making the trip from the mountains to our winter camp in fall. But now, the trails were covered with ice and snow. It would be a hard trip. My uncles prepared to leave.

There was no dancing in my eyes as they took GrandGrand from his sleeping space. The warmest thing I owned was the white rabbit fur piece. I remembered what Father had said, that my old robe was warm enough for me. I knew that GrandGrand needed to stay warm on the journey, so I spread my rabbit fur robe over him. I watched as my

uncles strapped it around his weak
body and took him away.

There was more and more snow. My uncles did not return.

Families gathered for visiting and festivities in the winter. It was in the spring, at the first sound of thunder, that the Ute Bear Dance was held. It honored the grizzly bear.

The grizzly was created by the One-Above to teach the Ute strength, wisdom, and survival. The dance was to awaken the bear so he would lead us to roots, nuts, and berries.

GrandMama and Mother made clothes for us to wear to the festival. They spent extra time making large feather plumes.

"GrandMama, what are the plumes for?" I asked.

GrandMama said, "We wear the large feather plumes to the festival."

GrandMama continued, "They represent our worries. On the fourth day, we will hang them on a cedar tree at the east entrance of the corral. When we leave, we leave them there. This means we leave our troubles behind. One is for you, Chumani."

The day before the festival began, I took a walk to see the Earth as she began to open and let out her young. The sun was low in the sky. Away in the distance I saw four men.

One of the men had something white over his arm. Something white—could it be? It was! There came GrandGrand and my uncles, hurrying down the trail! I called to GrandMama and Mother. Then I ran toward the men.

When I reached GrandGrand, I stopped in front of him. He wrapped me in his arms.

GrandGrand smiled and said, "Thank you for loaning me your white rabbit fur piece, Chumani. Here, you may have it back."

GrandGrand placed the rabbit fur piece around my neck.

GrandGrand said, "I see the last rays of sun dancing in your eyes, my happy child."

Again, we stood together on the soft earth.

Four

Ute Facts

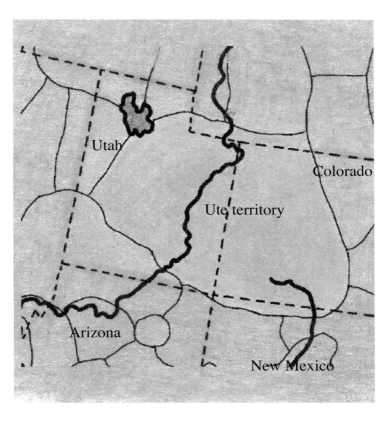

Above are three types of housing used by the
Ute tribes: Plains tepee and two forms of wickiup. The tepee was a rather recent style and
never as large or fancy as the tepees of the
Sioux.

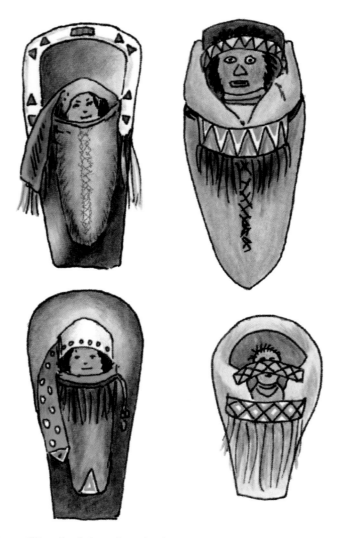

Two Ute babies in their cradleboards and two dolls in their cradleboards.

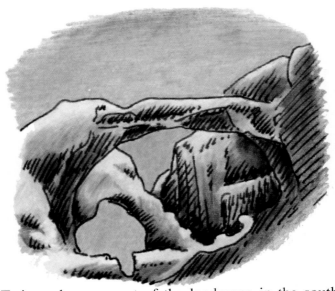

Twin arches are part of the landscape in the southern Ute area.

The Utes lived in a country filled with rock art. Tall cliffs were painted with tall red clay figures. The animals at right are petroglyphs. The figures were tapped deeply into the rock.

This is a younger and an older picture of Chief Ignacio of the Southern Utes. When the U.S. government pushed for the Utes to accept allotments, Chief Ignacio refused. He led his band to the Ute Mountain Reservation and kept it together as a tribe. This group was the last to live free and follow the old ways. He was later made a police chief of the reservation.

Ute war shield

Dance lodge used in the Bear Dance each spring.

Beyond "The End"

● What is in a name? The English borrowed many words, especially words for plants and animals, from Native American languages. A man by the name of Walt Whitman heard music in the Indian names. Half of our states took their names from Indian words.

Make a list of all the borrowed words. Here are a few to help you get started: persimmon, raccoon, moose, moccasin, totem, succotash, squash, and hominy. Was the name of your state derived from Native Nations?

CURRICULUM CONNECTIONS

● Historically, the Ute Nation roamed throughout what now is Colorado, northern New Mexico, Utah, and Arizona. Where are the homelands today for the bands within the Ute Nation?

● GrandGrand had absolutely no trouble knowing the white-tailed jackrabbit in the winter. Do you know how to distinguish between the black-tailed jack and the white-tailed jack in the summer?

● In Ute society, arrow and spearhead makers held a special place of honor. What jobs in America today do you think are especially honorable?

● What is the Continental Divide? It passes through Colorado.

● Visit some of Colorado's many caves on the Internet. Listen to the winds in the Cave of the Winds at <www.caveofthewinds.com>. While there, look at "Caving Tips" and "Kid's Activities". Find information about the sacred cave where GrandGrand was taken—Yampa.

● The bear was admired for its strength and courage. A grizzly can weigh 1,000 pounds. How much more does a grizzly weigh than you?

● How would your life be different if you were a Ute instead of a Navajo; if you were a Cherokee rather than an Apache; if you were a Haida instead of a Blackfeet? How is your life different from a student your age on the Hopi Reservation?

THE ARTS

● Springtime was a time for a great celebration for the Utes. It all began with the Bear Dance. The bear-dance songs were performed to welcome the spring when the bear came out of hibernation. Hear music at <www.encarta.msn.com/encnet/refpages/RefMedia.aspx?refid=461524637>.

Dancing is usually in single lines or in parallel lines that face each other, with the two lines alternately meeting and receding.

Morache is a major instrument used. It is a notched stick, scraped with another stick.

Using these bear-dance songs, this dancing style, and a morache, create and dance a Ute Bear Dance.

GATHERING INFORMATION

● The Utes, and most Native Americans, lived in close family groups. Do you ever wonder about your family's history—who your ancestors are, where they came from, and such? This is called genealogical research. It is very interesting.

Keep this in mind. You have two families to consider—four families when you involve your grandparents. How many families are involved if you go back five generations? (32 families). If you go back 20 generations, you will be learning about your 1,048,576 family surnames!

Ask your mother to show you the family tree page in your baby book and/or the family Bible. Good luck!

THE BEST I CAN BE

● When you hear the words"Indian" or "Native American", what pictures come to mind? If you saw someone wearing feathers, living in a tipi, or making a "whooping" sound, you do not have an accurate portrayal of the rich and varied cultures of the American Indian. You should study the many differences and rare qualities of the individual tribes.

A good beginning in this study would be to read the twenty books in the Story Keeper Series. Make a chart to keep records of such things as climate, homes, foods, clothing, music, legends, and celebrations. Be the best you can be! Learn about the cultures of individual tribes.